Dear Parent

We believe that children are a
gift from God and that helping
them learn and grow is nothing less
than a divine privilege.

With that in mind, we hope these
"Veggiecational" books provide years
of rocking chair fun as they teach
your kids fundamental concepts
about the world God made.

– *Phil Vischer*

President
Big Idea Productions

More Veggiecational Fun!

by Phil Vischer

Tommy NELSON™

Thomas Nelson, Inc.
Nashville

More Veggiecational Fun!

features these Veggiecational stories

Archibald's Opposites

by Phil Vischer

Time for Tom

by Phil Vischer

ARCHIBALD'S OPPOSITES
Art Direction: Ron Eddy
3D Illustrator: Aaron Hartline

TIME FOR TOM
Art Direction: Ron Eddy
3D Illustrator: Aaron Hartline
Assistant 3D Illustrator: Jeremy Vickery

Library of Congress Cataloging-in-Publication Data
Vischer, Phil.
    More veggiecational fun / by Phil Vischer.
    p. cm.
  Two books in one.
  Previously published separately in 1998.

  ISBN 0-8499-7531-X
    1. Children's stories, American. [1. English language--Synonyms and antonyms Fiction. 2. Time Fiction. 3. Clocks and watches Fiction. 4. Vegetables Fiction. 5. Grapes Fiction. 6. Short stories. 7. Stories in rhyme.] I. Vischer, Phil. Archibald's opposites. 1999. II. Vischer, Phil. Time for Tom. 1999. III. Title: Archibald's opposites IV. Title: Time for Tom. V. Title.
  PZ8.3.V74 Mo 1999
  428.1--dc21
                       99-32496
                       CIP

Printed in the United States of America

99 00 01 02 03 BVG 9 8 7 6 5 4 3 2

Archibald's Opposites

by Phil Vischer

Good morning dear class —
Archibald is my name!

Today we'll be playing
the Opposites Game!

What's that you say?
    Oh, you don't know that word —
You think it sounds silly, or weird or absurd?

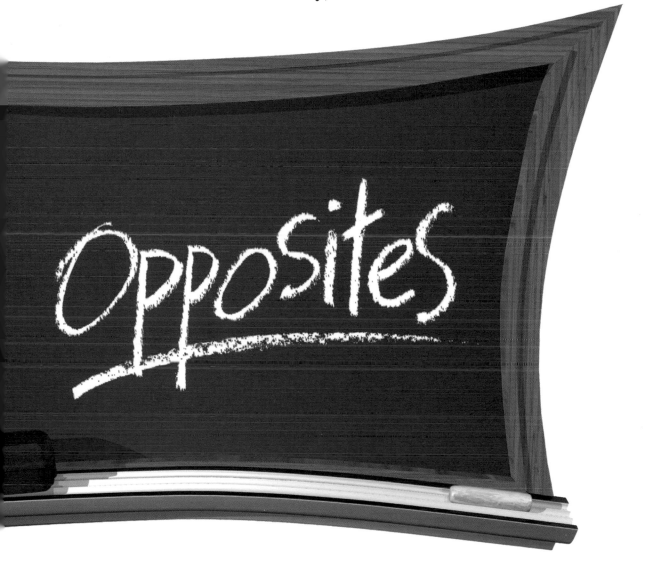

I'm happy to say that I've traveled quite far
To teach you exactly what opposites are!

Here on the board I have drawn a small pea.
(Especially small, since he's not even three!)

Next on the board, and I've drawn him in yellow,
Is mighty Goliath! A very big fellow!

When things are as different
    as different can be,
We call them opposites! Now do you see?

Yes, **little** and **big**. But please, hold your cheers!
To show you some more, I'll need two volunteers!

Ah! Here they are now, and I'm thrilled to report —
The green one is **tall** and the red one is **short**!

See? More opposites!
Isn't it grand?
But I can do more
so that you'll understand.

This is a sunlamp to make Larry bright.
But over by Bob, it's as dark as the night!

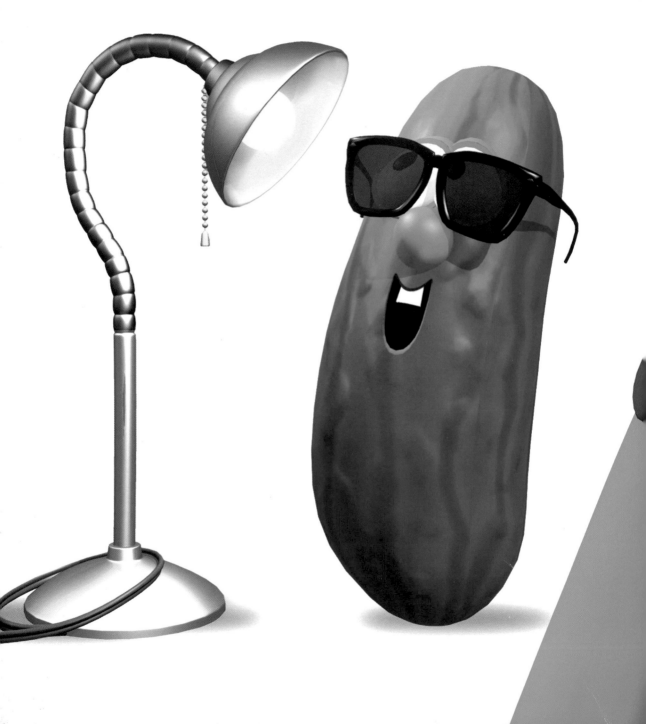

Yes, **light** and **dark**!
   Oh, now isn't this fun?
Don't go away, please.
   Our game isn't done!

The sunlamp will also make Larry quite **hot**.
Think of the opposite. What have you got?

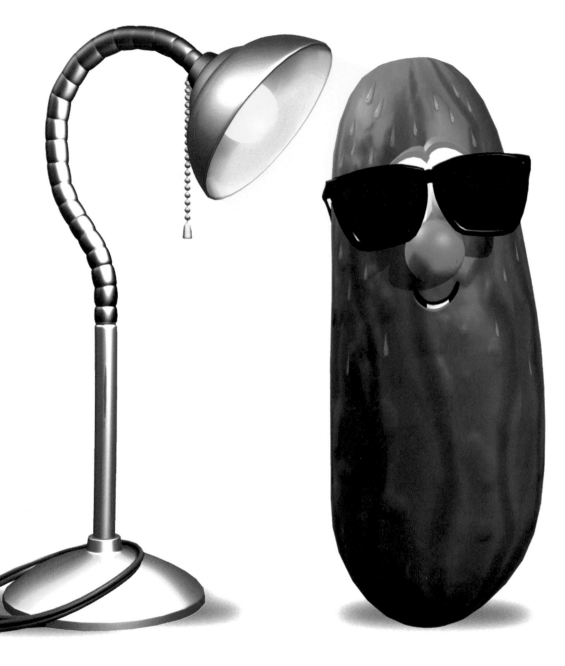

Cold is the word! Is that what you said?
Let's make Bob cold. We'll put ice on his head!

Hmm, **hot** and **cold**. Now, that makes me think
Of delicious iced tea and hot cocoa to drink!

The tea is for Larry.
   He thinks it's yummy!
Bob gets the cocoa
   to warm his red tummy!

But wait...

I've taken Bob's cocoa and now he feels blue!
Happy and **sad**. Those are opposites, too!

Next I'll give Larry a **sweet** chocolate pie —
While Bob gets a **sour** old lemon to try!

Hmm . . .

Someone's unhappy . . .
   and Bob is his name.
Perhaps he's not liking
   my Opposites Game?

He's coming right at me! Oh, dear — this is scary!
I think he's forgetting that pie was for Larry!!

One final lesson
  before we are through —
Dirty and **clean**.
  These are opposites, too.

Time for Tom

by Phil Vischer

Bob and Larry are here today
To stage for you a little play.
So call your dad and get your mom —
It's time to start "It's Time for Tom!"

It's time for Tom
    to rise and shine.
The sun is up;
    he's feeling fine!

The bus will come at five till nine.
It's time for Tom to rise and shine.

It's time for Tom
     to make his bed
And fluff the pillow
     that holds his head

And smooth the sheet with the purple thread.
It's time for Tom to make his bed.

It's time for Tom
to go to school
And learn about
the golden rule

And sit at his desk
on a tiny stool.
It's time for Tom
to go to school.

It's time for Tom
to eat his lunch
With Laura and Junior,
his favorite bunch.

With things to drink, and things to munch,
It's time for Tom to eat his lunch.

It's time for Tom
to play outside —
To run and jump
and swing and slide,

With places for Junior
    and Laura to hide!
It's time for Tom
    to play outside.

It's time for Tom to eat again,
With Ma and Pa
they sit and then

Thank God for their food with a big Amen!
It's time for Tom to eat again.

It's time for Tom to hit the tub.
From head to toe,
    he needs a scrub!

So get the soap and start to rub.
It's time for Tom to hit the tub!

It's time for Tom
to go to bed.
He's feeling tired —
his eyes are red.

He puts his nightcap on his head.
It's time for Tom to go to bed.

It's time for Tom
to say his prayers.
He's thankful for
a God who cares —

Who fills us up with the love He shares.
It's time for Tom to say his prayers.

It's time for Tom
to say good night.
Pa tucks him in —
turns out the light.

He'll start again when the sun is bright.
It's time for Tom to say good night.

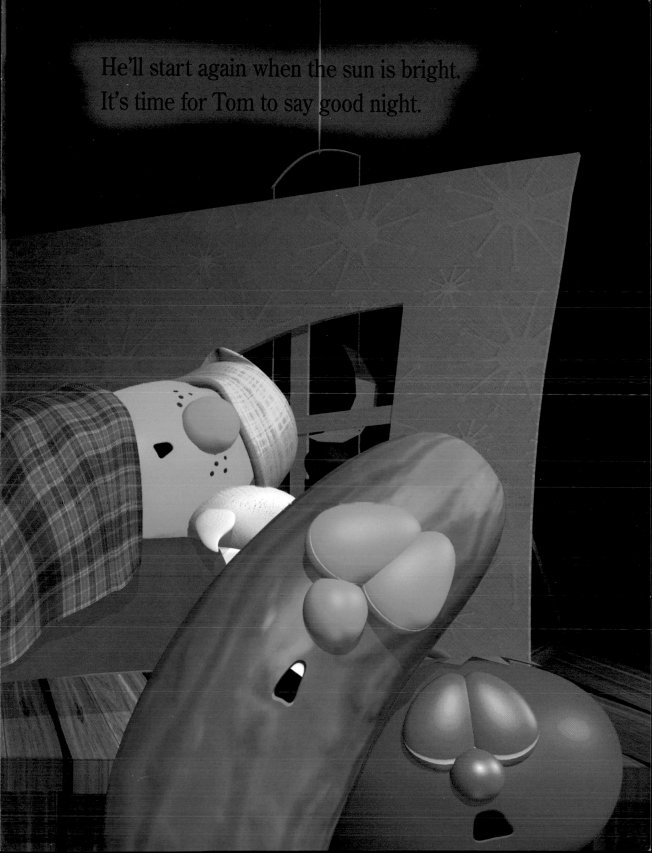